MELTING POTS
Family Stories and Recipes

Judith Eichler Weber

Illustrated by
Scott Gubala

SILVER MOON PRESS
New York

First Silver Moon Press Edition 1994

Copyright © 1994 by Judith Eichler Weber
Illustration copyright © 1994 by Scott Gubala

For information contact:
Silver Moon Press
126 Fifth Avenue
Suite 803
New York, NY 10011
(800) 874-3320

Design: Jacqueline Ho and Geoffrey Notkin
Project Editor: Bonnie Bader

Library of Congress Cataloging-in-Publication Data

Weber, Judith Eichler, 1938-
Melting pots: family stories and recipes/
by Judith Eichler Weber. – 1st ed.
p. cm. – (Family Ties)
ISBN 1-881889-53-X : $11.95
1.Cookery, International – Juvenile literature
2. Food habits – Juvenile literature
[1. Cookery, International. 2. Food habits.]
I. Title. II. Series: Family ties (New York, NY)
TX725.A1W363 1994
641.59–dc20
93-42507

10 9 8 7 6 5 4 3 2 1
Printed in the USA

TABLE OF CONTENTS

Celebrating With Food

LOTS OF POTS

It is always fun to celebrate a special occasion with our family or friends – like a birthday, an anniversary, or a holiday.

At some celebrations, we're asked to bring gifts. At others we're asked to wear a costume. But no matter what the celebration, there's always FOOD! At a birthday party, we might eat cake. At a family barbecue, we might eat grilled hot dogs and hamburgers. On Thanksgiving, we may gobble turkey.

Often the food we eat at family celebrations relates to where our families originally came from – our ethnic heritage. If your family heritage is Russian, you might like to eat borscht and stuffed cabbage. If your family heritage is Japanese, you might like to eat miso soup and tempura.

Our country was once thought to be a melting pot where people of different cultures could blend together. But it might now be more accurate to describe our country as a place that plays home to many melting pots. People want to keep their special celebrations and customs. The many melting pots of food have led to a wide variety of restaurants. There's probably an Italian pizza parlor, a Greek diner, a Japanese sushi bar, or a Mexican restaurant in your own neighborhood.

Melting Pots is a book about the different ways people celebrate with food. You will learn what Chinese people eat during their New Year celebrations. You will also read about Greek, African-American, English, and Cuban families and the special foods they have brought to this country.

So get ready to start your journey into the world of food. When you're finished reading the stories, you can put on your own chef's hat and try your hand at cooking!

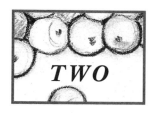

TWO

Family Parties

THE CHERRY PIES

Many families get together for holidays, such as Thanksgiving, Independence Day, Christmas, or Chanukah. But families don't only get together at holiday times. Sometimes family members don't live near each other, so they have family reunions to bring everyone together. Family reunions are a joyful time. At some family reunions, people dance and sing. At others, grandparents and parents tell the children stories. But maybe best of all, family reunions offer a chance to taste many delicious family recipes.

At some family gatherings, recipes from different countries are prepared. For example, at a family reunion where the people have a Polish background, Polish food, such as pierogi – dumplings stuffed with special fillings – may be served.

Or, in Hawaii, families may have luaus, or cookout parties, during their reunions. At some luaus, families bake a whole pig in an underground oven called an imu. A starchy food, called poi, made from a plant root, might also be served. It's eaten instead of potatoes or rice. And at luaus, many different local fruits are eaten, such as papaya, mango, and pineapple.

In the story "The Cherry Pies," the Phillips family is preparing for a big annual picnic called the Cousins Club. Members of the family come from all over to attend the party. This year relatives are coming from England! What makes the Cousins Club special is that everyone brings their favorite dishes made from family recipes. That seems like an easy task, but for the Phillips family, things don't quite work out according to plan...

Peter Manik

For families like the Maniks, making apple pies gets everyone involved with what's happening in the mixing bowl as well as the melting pot.

4

"I can smell the pies!" ten-year-old Kevin Phillips shouted as he ran up the gravel driveway to the farm house.

"Cherry pies!" seven-year-old B.J. said as he followed his older brother. "Ma must be baking for the Cousins Club party."

When Kevin reached the porch, he took a deep breath and thought about the sweet taste of cherry pie. He imagined biting into a slice, and sinking his teeth into a juicy cherry. Yum!

Kevin opened his eyes and looked at the pies, which were sitting on the kitchen window ledge. Ma always left the pies there to cool. He counted them carefully. "There are only six," he announced.

"There should be seven," B.J. said with a frown. "Six for all the relatives to eat at the party and one for us to eat tonight. That's what Ma bakes every year."

Kevin picked up one pie, sniffed the sweet aroma, and carried it into the house. "Ma! Anyone home?"

No one answered.

The boys walked into the kitchen. "There's a note on the table," Kevin said. He read it aloud. *"Kevin & B.J., Please do not eat the pies. They are for the Cousins Club tomorrow. I ran out of cherries, so I couldn't make an extra pie. There's homemade applesauce in the refrigerator to eat. I'll be back at five. Love, Ma."*

"Applesauce! Yuck!" B.J. said. Kevin put the pie on the table. It was nine inches in diameter, and topped with a light brown crust with tiny holes in it. Ma always pierced the crust with a fork so that the heat could come out.

B.J.'s mouth was watering. "I've got to have a taste," he said.

"Me, too," agreed Kevin. "But remember the note Ma wrote. We'll be in big trouble if we take a piece."

"Just a tiny taste," B.J. said. He broke off a piece of crust. "Mm—the crust is good, but I want to taste the cherries."

"I've got an idea." Kevin took a blunt butter knife and a long-handled iced-tea spoon from the drawer. Carefully he worked the knife around half of the pie. "Quick, B.J., get a wooden spoon!"

Without breaking the crust, Kevin propped the wooden spoon under a small section. Then he slipped the smaller metal spoon under the crust and pulled out a big, juicy cherry.

"You're a genius!" B.J. said. He took a pie off the window ledge. Then he found his own utensils—a blunt knife, a wooden spoon, and iced-tea spoon—and dug in.

In half an hour, the boys had worked their way through the six pies. They had eaten as many cherries out of the pies as they could reach with their iced-tea spoons. As Kevin put the six pies back on the window sill, B.J. carefully washed the knives, wooden spoons, and iced-tea spoons. Then they went outside to play.

The boys were in the backyard when they heard their

mother calling. "Come clean up, boys!" she shouted.

Kevin and B.J. ran into the house and kissed Ma hello.

"I'm going to grill some hot dogs for dinner," Ma told the boys. "Outside," she added. "I'm beat from baking all morning and it's too warm to cook inside. I think Clover is the hottest place in Iowa –"

Suddenly, Ma stopped talking. Kevin looked at her. She was staring at the window ledge. Her eyes were wide with surprise. "What happened to my pies?!"

Kevin and B.J. looked over at the pies and gasped. The flaky crowns on all of the pies had collapsed. Instead of looking like pies, they looked like big brown bowls!

"All my pies caved in!" Ma exclaimed. She covered her mouth to hold back a cry. "This has never happened before." Gently she took one pie and placed it on the kitchen table. She turned the pie around and suddenly stopped. The slit made by the knife was facing her. "Who's been eating the filling out of these pies?"

The boys looked at each other.

Ma went to the drawer and took out her triangle-shaped pie knife. She cut a wedge. The crust completely flopped down. She scooped the piece out. "There's not one cherry left in this pie!" Ma said angrily.

"We're sorry," Kevin blurted out.

"What will I bring tomorrow to the Cousins Club?" Ma demanded. She inspected the other five pies. "Our relatives from London will be here and I promised I'd bake the family recipe for cherry pie." She glared at Kevin and B.J. "Go to your room!"

An hour later Kevin heard his father come into the house. He called Kevin and B.J. to come down the stairs.

"Boys, you're in big trouble," he said.

"I know," Kevin said sadly.

"We're sorry," B.J. added.

"Sorry isn't good enough. You're going to make pies tonight."

B.J. and Kevin looked blankly at their father. "But Ma wrote in her note that she doesn't have any cherries," Kevin said. "So we couldn't possibly make more cherry pies."

"But in the barn, I have bags of apples," their father began. "You'll make apple pies. And not just six pies. You're going to peel enough apples to bake twelve apple pies! Six are going to the Cousins Club party, and six you are going to give away to the church for their soup kitchen."

That night the boys peeled, and peeled, and peeled. Then they mixed, rolled, and baked. Their arms ached, and their backs grew tired. Ma watched their every move, but she didn't help them.

The next day was the big party. Grandma and Grandpa Phillips rented a covered picnic area in Clover Park since no one had a house large enough to hold all the relatives. Long wooden tables were covered with bright paper cloths, and each table had an arrangement of fresh flowers. All the cousins prepared food — chicken, potato salad, corn on the cob, and green salad. The desserts were placed together. Little cards with the names of the bakers were displayed next to their desserts.

Kevin and B.J. put their six apple pies behind their name card. The pie crusts were slightly uneven and the dough looked lumpy. But when their relatives tasted the pies, everyone said they were delicious.

"Next year," Kevin said to his brother, "let's make cherry pies."

"No way!" B.J. said. "It's too much work making pies. I'd rather eat them!"

"Okay," Kevin said with a grin, "but only if they're ours!" He and B.J. laughed.

Peter Manik

Using rolling pins and elbow grease, the Maniks keep their family bonds strong through piemaking.

THREE

Birthday Parties

THE NOODLE

We celebrate birthdays to mark the passing from one stage of life to another. In many cultures, someone who is twelve is still considered a child. But when that person's birthday rolls around, he or she becomes a teenager.

How did the custom of celebrating birthdays get started? Many, many years ago, people thought changes were dangerous – times when good and evil spirits came together. And since birthdays were a time of change, they were thought to be a bad thing. Birthday parties started because people believed that having friends and family around to express good wishes would protect the person having a birthday.

But not everyone celebrates birthdays. There are

tribes in the African Congo and Australia that do not keep a record of time. So they have no idea when it's someone's birthday!

Most people do celebrate birthdays. Families have different ways of celebrating. Some families celebrate half-birthdays. Other families have a party on the day a baby is given his or her name.

In Hungary, it is the custom to have two birthday celebrations, one on the day a person was born, and the second on a person's "official" name day. For example, if your name is Paula, you'd have your second celebration on March 9th, which is the official name day for all people with the name Paula!

Whenever a birthday is celebrated, there is food. Usually, a cake with candles is served at birthday parties. Each candle represents a year that the person has lived. There is sometimes an extra candle to make a wish for the coming year. But in order for all your wishes to come true, you have to blow out all the candles!

In many homes, people bake birthday cakes themselves. In an Italian home, a ricotta cheesecake might be served for a birthday. In a German home, Black Forest cake – a chocolate cake with cherries – might be served.

Although birthday cakes are common, traditional Asian families do not celebrate birthdays with cake. Instead, a special birthday noodle is served. The noodles are made out of flour. First they are boiled,

Geoffrey Notkin

Chinese families often gather together to prepare traditional foods that are rich in cultural meaning.

then they are fried and boiled again. Birthday noodles are very long and symbolize long life. Sometimes there is only one long noodle in a bowl, but other times there are many noodles, which symbolize many years of life.

"The Noodle" is the story of a Chinese-American girl who wonders if her grandmother has forgotten her birthday. But Grandmother has something very special planned.

*   *   *

Six-year-old Hua Chang sat quietly in her grandmother's kitchen. She was worried. She was afraid her grandmother would forget her birthday.

Hua lived with her mother and father in a suburb of San Francisco, California. But her parents had gone on a trip, so she had come to stay at Grandmother's apartment, in the Chinatown section of San Francisco.

Grandmother was busy preparing for the Chinese New Year's celebration. The four-day holiday is based on the lunar, or moon, calendar, and occurs between mid-January and the beginning of February. This year, Hua's seventh birthday fell during the New Year's holiday.

"Hua, come help me prepare for the New Year's banquet," Grandmother said in Chinese. She unwrapped a giant fish with head and tail. "Everything must be eaten whole," she added.

"Why?" Hua asked, staring at the fish head and tail.

"To show that everything is complete and whole. Little Flower, your mother has not taught you the Chinese traditions. While you are staying with me, you will be a Chinese granddaughter."

Hua stood on a chair and washed the vegetables: bok choy, pea pods, and cabbage. She didn't know the Chinese words for "birthday party." Her grandmother didn't speak English, so Hua was very worried.

The second night Hua was at her grandmother's, it was the Chinese New Year's Eve. There was a grand banquet. Many relatives came who Hua did not know. Grandmother served a whole roast pig and a whole fish. Aunt Lian brought a special dessert eaten only at holidays. It was very sweet and reminded Hua of firm pudding. Hua wondered if Grandmother would make the dessert for her birthday.

The next day, Grandmother was up early. Hua joined her in the kitchen, where Grandmother was busy cooking. "Only dumplings are eaten on New Year's Day," Grandmother told Hua.

"Why do we eat dumplings?" Hua asked. She was helping Grandmother fill the square pieces of dough with ground meat and chopped shrimp.

"Look at the shape of the dumpling," Grandmother said. She held up the little round bundle. "It is in the shape of old coins and represents money and prosperity." Grandmother said nothing about Hua's birthday. She only talked about the dumplings.

The third day, the family only ate noodles. "The noodles represent long life," Grandmother told Hua. She did not say anything about Hua's birthday. Hua was more than worried now. She was sad. They were going to miss her birthday!

The next day was Hua's seventh birthday. When Hua woke up, there was a big package on her bed. On the top was a letter from her parents. *They* had remembered her birthday! Inside the box was a bright pink jacket. Hua put on the jacket over her nightgown and went into the kitchen. Grandmother was chopping vegetables.

"What a pretty jacket!" Grandmother said. "Now, you must get dressed, Little Flower. Our relatives are coming for a New Year's celebration."

The relatives ate everything that was left over from the first three days. Just before they left, Grandmother brought out a giant bowl.

"Why, a fish could swim in that bowl," Uncle Tao said.

"I could bathe my baby in that bowl," Aunt Lian added.

Grandmother put the bowl in front of Hua.

Hua peered inside.

"It is your birthday noodle," Grandmother said proudly.

All the relatives gathered around Hua and the bowl. They looked at the coils of noodle.

"When your parents come back, you will have an American birthday party," Grandmother said. "But while you are staying with me, you will have a Chinese birthday!" Grandmother gave Hua chopsticks. "It is an old Chinese custom to make a very long noodle for a birthday," she explained. "The noodle brings you a long life."

The family wished Hua a happy birthday and long life. Hua tried to eat the noodle, but it was too long to finish.

Hua smiled. Grandmother *had* remembered her birthday, and in a special way. "I have had birthday cake every year, Grandmother, but this is my first birthday noodle!"

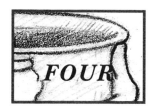

School Parties

BEAN SOUP

Many parties take place in school – Halloween parties, Valentine's Day parties, sometimes even birthday parties.

Sometimes schools throw special parties, like international fairs. At these events people bring foods that represent their ethnic heritage. When you walk through an international fair, your eye catches many new and interesting dishes. And your nose picks up many new and delicious smells!

At some school parties, you are asked to bring a dish from home. Every student brings a different food, so you get to sample all kinds of new foods. At other school parties, the food is cooked at the school. Students may even get to help cook.

In the story "Bean Soup," Elena and Sofia Karos want to make a Greek bean soup for their school's fair, but they run into some trouble along the way.

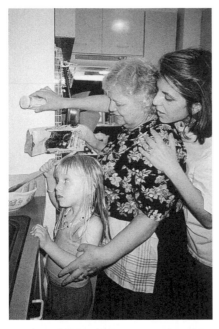

Left:
Tess Leverenz, her mother, Beverley Shenkman Leverenz, and Tess' grandmother, Beatrice, put three sets of hands in the pot to make a Greek bean soup.

Bottom:
Family celebrations are happy times — especially in the kitchen.

Photos by the author

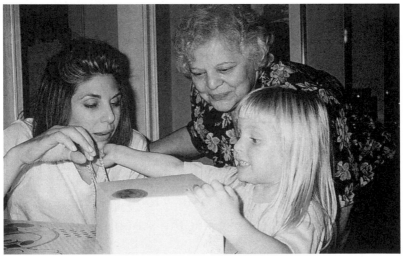

"Look, Elena!" seven-year-old Sofia Karos shouted. She ran from the school building toward a tall, dark-haired girl. "There's going to be a school food fair." Sofia pressed the notice into her older sister's hand.

Fourteen-year-old Elena read the note. *"The P.T.A. is sponsoring an international food fair. On Friday, please send to school a family specialty for your child's classmates to share."*

"I want to make one of our Greek dishes," Sofia said as they neared their apartment house.

"What kind of dish?" Elena asked, as she unlocked the apartment door. Elena took care of her younger sister after school, while their parents worked at a grocery store.

Sofia didn't answer her sister, and instead ran straight into the kitchen. She opened the cupboard and stared at the shelves. Suddenly she saw the bags of beans. *"Fasolada!"* she shouted. "That's what we'll bring."

"Bean soup?" Elena asked.

"White bean soup. I'm sure it's easy to make," Sofia said. "I've watched Mama make it."

"How will you bring the soup to school?" Elena asked.

"Easy. I'll use the big, two-quart thermos jug. And I can bring paper cups to serve the soup in."

Elena took down the bag of beans and read the directions. "It says to soak the beans overnight. Tomorrow we can make the soup and Friday we'll take it to school."

"I think we should make all the bags of beans," Sofia

said. "There are a lot of kids at school to feed." She took three large bags of beans from the shelf.

Elena and Sofia filled a big spaghetti pot and a large soup pot with water. Then they poured two bags of beans into the big pot and one bag into the smaller pot.

Elena cooked dinner for Sofia. Then she helped Sofia with her homework. The girls were in bed when their parents came home from working at the store. Elena had forgotten to leave their parents a note about the bean soup.

The next morning, Sofia and Elena woke to Mama's shouts.

"Oh! Oh, no! Help!" Mama cried.

"What is it?" Papa called.

The sisters jumped out of their beds and ran to the kitchen door. "What's wrong, Mama?"

Mama was standing in the center of the kitchen. She was pointing to the stove.

"Beans!" Mama said.

"They're everywhere!" Papa shouted. Elena's eyes popped open. Plump, white beans were flowing over the tops of the two pots on the stove. Streams of beans were running down into a puddle of beans that was spreading across the kitchen floor.

"Get more pots!" Mama ordered.

"I'll get the mop!" Papa said.

Sofia started to cry. "My beans!"

Mama ladled beans from the two pots into smaller

ones. "I'll get a pail!" Elena offered frantically. The pool of beans on the floor continued to spread.

Everyone was working to clean up the kitchen. Soon every pot and bowl was filled with beans, but all the spilled beans had to be thrown out.

Mama washed the floor. "Girls, what happened? Why did you make so many beans?"

Sofia told her parents about the food fair.

Mama started to laugh, followed by Papa.

Elena and Sofia didn't laugh. What was so funny? "Are you angry with us?" Sofia asked.

"Don't worry, little one. You didn't know that beans get bigger and bigger when you soak them. They drink up all the water," Mama explained.

"What will we do with all these beans?" Elena said.

"We'll make bean soup this afternoon when you come home from school. I'll borrow pots from Aunt Anna's restaurant," Mama said.

"What will we do with so much bean soup?" Papa asked. "I'll be an old man before we eat it all!" He laughed.

"Don't worry. Good soup is easy to give away," Mama said.

After school, Mama, Elena, and Sofia made many pots of bean soup. Mama filled two big red thermos jugs for the school food fair, then she put soup in plastic containers and placed them in her freezer.

"What will we do with the rest of the soup?" Elena

looked at the four giant pots still on the stove. They had worked all afternoon and into the evening.

"You'll see," Mama said. "Now let's have a bowl of soup."

At exactly eight o'clock the doorbell rang. Elena answered the intercom. "It's our aunts – all four of them."

"Buzz them up!" Mama said.

When Elena and Sofia opened the apartment door, their four aunts were crowding the hallway in front of the door. Each one was carrying a shopping bag. Inside the bags were containers.

Mama ladled the soup into the containers. There was laughing and talking. Mama told them about the beans that would not stop growing.

As they were leaving, the aunts hugged Elena and Sofia.

"You make delicious soup, but too much," Aunt Anna said. "What will you do with the rest of the soup?" she asked Elena and Sofia.

"Why, take it to a soup kitchen!" Elena answered.

FIVE

Surprise Parties

JAMBALAYA

Surprise parties can celebrate anything – birthdays, anniversaries, the arrival of a newborn baby, departures, or homecomings. The guest of honor never knows anything about the party. All the guests have to keep the event a secret.

Surprise parties are not popular in all countries. For instance, in traditional Japanese society there are no surprise parties. The Japanese do not like anything that disrupts the normal flow of activity. And since a surprise party does just that, it wouldn't be very popular. Of course, some people in Japan may still throw surprise parties.

No matter what occasion a surprise party celebrates, there is always food! And many times the food that is served reflects an ethnic heritage.

In the story "Jambalaya," Monique Washington and her brother and sister want to throw a surprise birthday party for their grandma. The Washingtons are an African-American family living in Louisiana. The children decide to use Creole recipes for the party. Creole cooking originated in Louisiana when Africans were brought over to be slaves on southern plantations. It was their exotic seasoning, combined with French, Spanish, and Native American cooking, that created Creole dishes such as jambalaya, gumbo, red beans and rice, and grits.

Monique and her younger siblings are trying to surprise their grandma with their cooking, but they just might be the ones who are in store for a surprise.

*   *   *

"I've got the key," ten-year-old Jonas Washington said. He removed the key from the string around his neck and opened the door to Grandma's cabin. Nothing stirred in the small house when he stepped in. His older sister Monique and his younger sister Honey followed him into the quiet cabin.

"Ugh, it's boiling hot in here," Jonas said. He quickly opened the front windows.

"I'll turn on the fan," Monique said. "We have to get to work. We have a lot to do before Grandma gets home."

Today was Grandma Lillie's seventieth birthday.

Monique, Jonas, and Honey were determined to make a wonderful surprise party. They wanted to cook Grandma's favorite foods – a seafood casserole called "jambalaya" and sweet potato bread, which are both Creole recipes. Many relatives were expected at Grandma's cabin tonight for the surprise birthday dinner. Mama was driving Grandma to Baton Rouge, Louisiana for the day so that she wouldn't see any of the preparations.

Monique carried two shopping bags of groceries into Grandma's kitchen. Mama had done the shopping while Monique, Jonas, and Honey were at school. "We'll have to hurry. Everyone is coming at six o'clock. Do you have the recipes, Honey?" Monique asked.

"Yes. Mama put them in my bag," eight-year-old Honey said. She was carrying the sack of paper decorations.

They unpacked all the bags, then started to work on the dinner. Monique cleaned the shrimp for the jambalaya, Jonas peeled the sweet potatoes, and Honey set the table with birthday plates and napkins.

Monique knew she was supposed to chop onions, scallions, and peppers for the jambalaya, but she wasn't sure what to do after that. "Honey, please get the recipes," Monique called.

Honey looked in the bag. The recipes were not there. She turned the bag upside down and shook it. Nothing fell out. "They're not here!" she cried.

"What?" Monique said.

"They have to be there," Jonas said.

Monique ran over to Honey and examined the shopping bag. "Maybe the recipes are in the other bags." She looked into all the bags.

"They're empty! How can we cook without recipes?" Monique cried.

"Don't worry," Jonas said. "We'll call Mama. She can read them to us."

Monique shook her head. "We can't. Mama took Grandma to Baton Rouge today, remember? We can't reach her."

"I know what we can do," Jonas said. He walked over to the kitchen phone. "I'll call Aunt Millie. She knows the recipes."

Jonas dialed Aunt Millie's number. The phone rang and rang. "No one's home," Jonas said glumly.

Honey started to cry. "What are we going to do?"

Monique took a deep breath. "Well, I guess we'll just have to try to cook and hope for the best," Monique said. "I've watched Grandma and Mama cook jambalaya and potato bread lots of times. I'll get Grandma's biggest pot for the jambalaya."

The three children mashed the sweet potatoes. Then they added the flour, brown sugar, eggs, cream, and spices to the mashed potatoes. Monique tasted the dough and shrugged. "It tastes all right. Jonas, grease the loaf pan."

"How long should we bake it?" Jonas asked.

"I'm not sure. But we can keep looking at it until it turns brown on top."

After they finished the sweet potato bread, the children put the vegetables, seasonings, and shrimp for the jambalaya in the big pot.

"It needs rice and water," Honey said.

"I know – but I don't know how much," Monique admitted nervously.

"Let's follow the recipe on the rice box," Jonas suggested.

"Good idea," Monique said.

The children put up the decorations while the food was cooking. Monique kept looking into the oven to check the bread. Finally, she said, "It looks ready!"

At six o'clock their father and Aunt Millie and her children came to the cabin. They brought the birthday cake.

"Don't tell anyone about the missing recipes," Monique ordered.

Jonas and Honey agreed.

Soon the living room was filled with relatives. "I think I hear the car," Aunt Millie said. "Everyone hide! Put out the lights, children."

The house was silent. The only sound was a key turning in the door. As the lights came on, everyone jumped up. "Surprise! Surprise!" they shouted. "Happy birthday!"

Grandma's face lit up. "Oh, what a wonderful surprise!" Grandma kissed everyone.

After Grandma opened her gifts, Monique put the food on the table. "We cooked everything," she said nervously to her Grandmother.

They watched carefully as Grandma took the first taste. "Why, this is delicious! I believe it's better than my recipe!"

"We made it up," Honey said. Then she clapped a hand over her mouth. "Oh, I shouldn't have told!"

"Told me what, little one?" Grandma said.

"We couldn't find the recipes Mama put in my bag, so Monique made up her own," Honey said.

Grandma hugged Monique. "You have the gift! Great chefs never follow a recipe. They make it up as they go along." All the relatives applauded.

Monique just smiled.

Two members of the author's family, her mother-in-law, Alice and her daughter-in-law, Stacey, cook a family favorite — stuffed cabbage.

Photo by the author

SIX

Bon Voyage Parties

FRIED PLANTAINS

Parting from a friend or a place can make some people feel sad. Although they might be excited about the new city or school or house they're going to, inside there might be a feeling of uneasiness.

Bon Voyage parties are a way to make people feel better about leaving. Bon voyage is a French phrase meaning "good trip." A bon voyage party was traditionally given for people taking long boat trips.

Going-away parties can be given for different reasons: changing schools, moving to a new city, going on a trip. You don't necessarily have to go on a ship or speak French in order to have a Bon Voyage party.

The story of Fried Plantains takes place in 1961 in Havana, Cuba. The Delgado family is leaving for the United States. The night they depart, the relatives staying behind give them a going-away party they won't soon forget.

*   *   *

It was a hot summer evening in 1961. The Delgado family was leaving on a secret flight from Cuba to the United States in a few hours. The government in Cuba had changed and many Cubans felt they had lost some of their freedoms. The Delgados didn't want to live in Cuba anymore.

Uncle Louis drove the pick-up truck to the Delgado house. Mama, Papa, brother Tomas, and seven-year-old Serita climbed into the back of the truck with all their cousins. Usually they would all talk and giggle, but this evening no one spoke. They were sad to be leaving Cuba, though they were happy to be going to the United States.

They drove a few miles to Grandmama's farmhouse. Grandmama had prepared a great feast for the entire family. There were more than fifty relatives crowded into her house and yard. Serita loved the smell of tomatoes and spices that filled the house. She saw a giant pot of moros, rice and black beans, on the stove. The table was filled was Cuban tamales, roast pork, sweet rice pudding, fresh fruits, and vegetables.

The family ate and talked. Serita played with her cousins. She was going to miss them a lot, and wondered when she would see them again.

After the party was over, Grandmama packed food in

a box for the plane trip. Just before Serita left, Grandmama took out a tray of fried plantains.

"This is your favorite dessert," Grandmama said. "I saved them especially for you."

"Will there be fried plantains in New York City?"

"Yes, Serita, but you will also eat things like hot dogs and ice cream," Uncle Louis said.

Grandmama cried. "You are so lucky to be going to America, but I will miss you."

Serita felt sad. "I will miss you, too. Please come to America with us."

"I can't, Serita," she said. "I am too old to leave my home."

As Serita climbed back into the truck, Grandmama handed her a little box. "Keep this in your sack and open it when you are lonesome for Cuba," Grandmama said.

Serita looked at the box. She wondered what was inside. Should she open it now? No, she would wait until she was lonesome for Cuba, like Grandmama said.

Uncle Louis drove the family to the airport. The official at the gate said he couldn't go inside, so they said goodbye in the truck.

Inside the airport, Serita waited in long lines. There were many men in uniforms with rifles. The Delgado family stood in the lines for hours. A soldier looked inside Serita's red cloth sack. He took out Grandmama's box. He opened it, smiled, and handed it to Serita's mother.

"I'll keep it with me," Mama whispered.

The family spent the night at the airport waiting for their flight. They were searched and questioned by officials. They had to leave everything behind except the clothes on their backs and a small bag of family photographs. Serita's father told her that they were lucky to get out of Cuba because they wouldn't have been allowed to live as they used to.

Finally in the morning they left for Miami, Florida. When Serita arrived in Miami, there were more lines and more waiting. Officers inspected their immigration papers. That night, Serita and her family boarded another airplane to New York.

In New York, the family was met by Papa's relatives. "This is your Uncle Jose and Aunt Rosa," Papa said excitedly. Uncle Jose was Serita's father's brother. There was a lot of hugging and talking.

Serita was hungry. Uncle Jose bought her her first American food from a stand at the airport – a hot dog! Serita liked it.

There were so many new things. A new apartment, strange words, and different foods.

The first Sunday, Serita and her family went to church. The priest spoke Spanish. Suddenly Serita felt very sad. In Cuba on Sundays the family always went to Grandmama's house after Mass. Tears came to her eyes.

"You look so sad," Papa said.

"I miss Grandmama," Serita answered.

"Would you like the box Grandmama gave you?" Mama asked. "I have saved it for you."

Serita had forgotten about the gift. "Yes," she said.

As soon as Serita returned to the apartment, Mama took her to the closet in the hall. On the top shelf was the little box. Mama took it down and handed it to her. What could be inside? Serita wondered. Carefully, she opened it. It was filled with pieces of paper!

"Mama! I can't read all the words on the papers," Serita said sadly. She handed the box to her mother.

Mama took out the crumpled papers. She smiled. Tears came to her eyes.

"These are your Grandmama's recipes. She wrote them down so that you'll be able to cook her food. Fried plantains and moros."

"Mama, can we cook together?"

"Yes, and we'll use Grandmama's recipes. Tonight our meal will be just like the food at her house."

By nightfall, the Delgado apartment smelled exactly like Grandmama's house in Cuba. The food tasted delicious. Serita felt as though her Grandmama was with them!

"Thank you, Grandmama," Serita whispered, even though she knew her grandmother couldn't hear her. "Eating your food has made me feel – at home!" she added with a smile.

Melting Pot Recipes

MAKE YOUR OWN MEALS

Now it's your turn to cook! A good way to start is with family recipes. Here are some tips:

- Ask your parents and relatives for favorite recipes.
- Ask to watch a recipe being prepared.
- Decide which recipe you'd like to cook.
- Plan a cooking session.

Once you've collected recipes, it's fun to create your own family cookbook.

- Write down the recipes.
- Put them in a binder.
- Add photographs or drawings.

The recipes from the stories in this book are on the following pages. But first, here are some safety tips. Remember always to:

•Wash and dry your hands before your start to cook.

•Ask an adult to help you when you are using the stove or oven.

•Use a potholder or side towel when handling pots and pans on the stove or in the oven. When you remove something from the oven put a potholder on one or on both hands. Never allow your potholders or sidetowel to get wet — water conducts heat!

•Use a wooden spoon or a spoon with a wooden or plastic handle. Metal spoons get very hot and can scratch good cookware!

•Place sauce pan and skillet handles away from you so that no one will bump into them and cause spills.

•Use a cutting board or butcher block when peeling, slicing, or chopping vegetables and fruits. It's best to have different cutting boards for different tasks — one for meat, one for poultry, one for fish, one for vegetables, and a nice big one for kneading dough.

•Peel in the direction away from you.

•Cut in a downward motion with your hand on top of the food, and always curl your fingertips in toward your palm.

Recipes

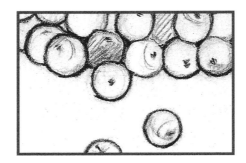

Apple Pie

At the end of "The Cherry Pies," Kevin and B.J. baked apple pies. Now you can make an apple pie, too! Instead of peeling and slicing the apples, the recipe suggests that you use canned apple slices. Be careful not to use apple filling – that will make the pie too sweet. The Phillips boys also made their own dough for all twelve pies. In this recipe, you can use frozen dough crusts.

Ingredients:

4 cups canned apple slices
2 frozen pie crusts
1/2 teaspoon cinnamon
3 tablespoons lemon juice
1 tablespoon margarine or butter
1/2 cup sugar
1/2 teaspoon nutmeg
2 tablespoons flour
pinch of salt

Utensils:

measuring spoons and cups
9-inch pie pan
knife
mixing spoon
large mixing bowl

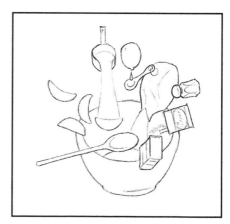

42

Preparation:

1. Preheat oven to 425° F.

2. Allow the frozen pie crusts to defrost in the foil tins. This can be done while you are making the filling.

3. Combine the canned apple slices, sugar, lemon juice, flour, salt, cinnamon, and nutmeg in the mixing bowl.

4. Leave one pie crust in its foil pan, and fill it with the apple mixture.

5. Put tiny pieces of margarine or butter on top of mixture.

6. Take the other pie crust out of its foil pan.

7. Carefully place it on top of the filled pie.

8. Press top crust to bottom around rim.

9. Cut slits in the top with a knife.

10. Bake for 45 minutes.

11. Cool on rack.

Dumplings

Chinese dumplings are fun to make, but it takes practice to get the little bundles just right. They are traditionally served on the second day of the Chinese New Year. This family recipe comes from the Ko family of New York.

Ingredients:

1/2 pound ground lean pork
1/2 cup cold water
1/2 cup soy sauce
2 to 3 teaspoons sesame oil
1/4 pound shelled and cleaned raw shrimp
1/2 pound fresh garlic cloves, peeled
1/4 cup peanut or vegetable oil
1 package of dumpling skins

Utensils:

large bowl
mixing spoon
chopping board
knife for chopping
measuring spoon
slotted spoon
large pot or Dutch oven
chopsticks or forks

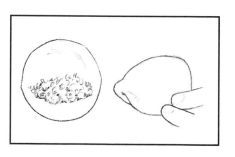

Preparation:

1. Chop shrimp.

2. Place pork in bowl. Add water, a little at a time. Mix.

3. Add shrimp, soy sauce, and peanut oil to pork. Mix.

4. Peel garlic cloves. Chop until fine. Add garlic to mixture.

5. Add sesame oil and blend.

6. Place a small amount of filling onto center of dumpling skin the long way. Fold and seal with a little water.

7. Boil water in large pot.

8. Place the dumplings into water one at a time.

9. Stir water with your chopstick to prevent dumplings from sticking to each other and to the pot.

10. Do not put too many dumplings into the water. Put lid on pot. Boil. Cook for two or three minutes or until they float to the top. Remove with slotted spoon or chopsticks.

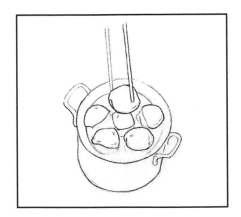

White Bean Soup

The Greek recipe for bean soup is simple, but don't double it or you'll be in trouble ... remember what happened to Elena and Sofia!

Ingredients:

2 pounds dried white beans
2 cubes chicken bouillon
1 pound potatoes (about 4)
1/4 cup tomato paste
1/2 teaspoon pepper
8 cups water
1/4 pound celery

Utensils:

large (8-quart) pot with cover
knife
measuring cup
soup ladle and soup bowls
long mixing spoon
cutting board

Preparation:

1. Cover beans with water and soak overnight in an 8-quart pot. Drain.

2. Put beans, bouillon cubes, pepper, and 8 cups of water in large pot. Bring to boil.

3. Lower heat, cover, and simmer for 1-1/2 hours.

4. Cut potatoes into quarters.

5. Cut celery.

6. Add potatoes and celery and cook for 1/2 hour more.

7. Add tomato paste and simmer for 15 minutes more.

8. Serve hot with crusty bread.

   (This recipe will serve 6 to 8 hungry people.)

Jambalaya

Jambalaya is a Creole recipe. You can use a combination of different seafood, chicken, or sausage. This is a one-pot dinner which will serve six to eight people. The cayenne and pepper are the spices that make it hot. The more cayenne you use, the spicier the dish.

Ingredients:

3 large onions, chopped
2 bell peppers, chopped
1 cup vegetable oil
1 8-ounce can tomato sauce
1 small can tomato paste
1/2 cup scallions, chopped
4 cups uncooked rice
1/2 cup parsley, chopped
2 cloves garlic, chopped
6 cups salted water
sprinkle of cayenne
sprinkle of pepper
2 pounds of cleaned shrimp (chicken and/or a mixture of seafoods can be substituted)

2 bay leaves

Utensils:

measuring cups and spoons
chopping board and knife
large frying pan
mixing spoon
large baking dish or casserole

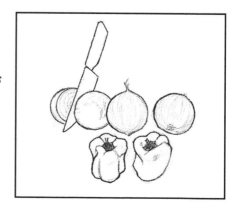

Preparation:

1. Chop onions and peppers.

2. Heat oil in frying pan.

3. Saute onions and peppers until you can see through the onions.

4. Add tomato sauce and paste.

5. Cover and cook for 3/4 hour over low heat.

6. Add remaining ingredients.

7. Stir well.

8. Bring to boil.

9. Pour mixture into large greased baking dish (rice will expand).

10. Bake at 300° F. for one hour.

11. Serve directly from baking dish.

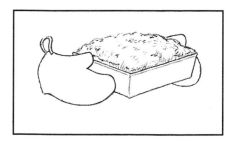

Fried Plantains

Fried plantains make a popular dessert in Cuba and Puerto Rico. If your green grocer or supermarket doesn't carry plantains, you can substitute green or firm bananas.

Ingredients:

6 plantains
1 cup peanut or vegetable oil
salt to taste

Utensils:

large frying pan
brown paper
spatula
serving dish

Preparation:

1. Peel the plantains.

2. Cut each into one-inch lengths.

3. Heat oil in frying pan.

4. Brown the plantains on both sides – about two minutes on each side.

5. Place on brown paper.

6. Sprinkle with salt.

Glossary

bok choy: a green leafy vegetable used in Asian cooking.

bon voyage: French for "have a good trip;" people say this when they want someone to enjoy a journey.

borscht: a beet soup that often includes meat.

Chinese New Year: A four-day holiday based on the lunar calendar. It falls between mid-January and the beginning of February.

Creole food: Highly seasoned food that comes from a combination of African, French, Spanish, and Native American traditions and often uses rice, okra, tomatoes, and peppers.

fasolada: a Greek white bean, often used to make soup.

grits: a cornmeal food usually boiled and served warm with butter, sugar, honey, or eggs. A staple of many breakfasts in the southern United States, grits can be found most often in white or cheese varieties and is served smooth as well as lumpy.

gumbo: Creole soup made with okra and other vegetables, and often with meat or seafood.

imu:

jambalaya: A rice dish made with ham, sausage, chicken, shrimp, or oysters, and seasoned with spices.

luau: A Hawaiian feast or cook-out.

miso (soup): A light, clear Japanese soup.

moros: A Cuban dish of rice and black beans.

pierogi: Polish dumplings stuffed with meat, cheese, or vegetable fillings.

plantain: A banana plant which has a greenish, starchy fruit.

poi: A starchy Hawaiian food made from the taro root.

sushi: Not just a food but a whole way of eating in Japan. Sushi takes a variety of raw fish and sea animals such as eels and squid and makes tasty, careful arrangements of them. The sushi chef is an expert at cutting the raw fish, combining it with packed rice, and placing it on special trays or wrapping it in small bundles called rolls. Sushi is eaten with chopsticks and with the fingers, and the pieces are usually dipped in spicy sauces.

tempura: Another Japanese cooking technique in which meats, seafood, and vegetables are lightly battered and then fried in pots of hot oil. The result is a tender food surrounded by a crispy crust.

The stories in this book are fiction, but they were inspired by interviews. I wish to thank the following people for their help. They made this book a true melting pot of cultures.

Claudina Delgado, Laura Stewart Harsch, Monique Kelly, Sheely Ko, Beverley Shenkman Leverenz, Paula Manik, Lillie McPherson, Maria E. Rodiquez, and Juliette Wilk-Chaffee.

'The Cherry Pies" section was inspired by my dear friend, Jane Ratcliffe Stewart, who passed away in June, 1993.

Jane Ratcliffe Stewart, cooking with her granddaughter, Caitlin

Melting Pots: Family Stories and Recipes, is dedicated with love to my daughter-in-law, Stacey Gillis Weber, with the hope that she will continue our family recipes and traditions.

JUDITH EICHLER WEBER

54